THE MERRY SHIPWRECK

By GEORGES DUPLAIX

Illustrated by TIBOR GERGELY

A GOLDEN BOOK • NEW YORK

LIFE was very peaceful on the barge.

Every morning Captain Barnacle would look at the East River and cock his weather eye. He knew whether it would rain before night.

When it did rain, the crew huddled around him while he spun a salty yarn about far-away places, shipwrecks, and oceans. Why, one would think the world was full of oceans!

On clear mornings, after Captain Barnacle had listened to all the Shipping News on the radio, he went off to market, and to chat with the crew's many friends ashore.

But one day, while Captain Barnacle was away, mother mouse crept into the galley. And while she ate a piece of cheese, her little mice were sharpening their teeth on the rope that held the barge fast to the pier.

Suddenly—before the parrot could say "Jack Robinson!"—the rope snapped, and the barge was heading down the river!

What a lark! All the animals hung over the side to wave good-by to Captain Barnacle, who was just coming back with his basket.

The cow steered, the donkey poled, and the pig waved a towel at all the tugs they passed.

They reached the end of the river, and traveling was such fun that no one noticed when the sun slipped under a cloud.

The sky grew dark. Soon there was thunder and lightning and wind and rain. Big waves slapped against the barge, rolling it this way and that.

The crew bellowed and barked and bleated and meowed
for dear life.

Finally, after tossing the helpless barge on a rock, the storm passed by. But there they were, shipwrecked and lost at sea, and very unhappy. Only the ducks didn't mind being soaking wet.

Many hours passed. At last they heard a boat whistle.

"Ship ahoy!" cried the parrot.

"Hurrah!" cried all the animals. "We're saved!"

Just then, the sun came out again and they saw a red Fireboat, which was coming to their rescue.

"Come aboard!" cried the Fire Chief.

And whom did they find on the boat but Captain Barnacle! He had been looking for them everywhere.

Soon they were scampering all over the Fireboat. The
donkey aimed the hose at the sky, the goat paraded the
deck in a fireman's hat and boots, and the hens roosted
on top of the red funnel.

Then, "Bong, bong, bong!" The cabin boy called everybody to dinner.

After dinner they went for a ride around the harbor,
past ferryboats, tugs, tankers, yachts, battleships,
rowboats, coal barges, liners, and freighters. But the
Fireboat, looking like a red-and-gold Circus Boat, was
far and away the finest of all.

At last everyone decided to have a look at the Statue of Liberty, and they sailed right up to it, landing on the little island underneath.

"Well, by cracky!" the keeper of the Statue of Liberty exclaimed. "Looks more like Noah's Ark than a Fireboat you've got there!"

On their way back they tied up alongside the battered barge. Poor Captain Barnacle looked very sad indeed.

"My poor barge!" he sobbed. "She was such a beautiful tub!"

"Never mind," said the Fire Chief. "Between your crew and mine we'll soon fix that!"

The firemen gave the animals lots of bright red paint, and a shiny brass bell to hang over the galley door. And they all went to work.

When everything was finished, Captain Barnacle was
pleased as punch. And so were the animals.

Then they thanked the firemen and clanged their new
bell for a last good-by.

The animals were so happy to go home that they sang and shouted all the way up the East River. They made so much noise that their friends on shore heard them, and hurried down to the dock.

The butcher was there, and the grocer, and the junkman with his horse.

The window cleaner, the mailman, the delivery boy, and the Good Humor man were there. So was Tony the fruit man—along with all the boys and girls and alley cats in the neighborhood.

"It's good to be home!" said Captain Barnacle, shaking hands around. "Let's have a party!"

"Yes, let's!" everybody shouted. "Hip, hip, hooray!"

They decorated the barge with Chinese lanterns, and Captain Barnacle cooked the best supper ever cooked in his little galley.

Just as he was ringing the bell, the firemen arrived and joined the party.

Before long, everyone was dancing around the deck, and singing songs in the moonlight.

And that night, while Captain Barnacle and his crew were dreaming rosy dreams, the little mice were also quietly asleep. They would never, never again sharpen their teeth on the rope that held them so safely to shore!